For Lena with love—A.L

Text copyright © 1998 by the Carl Sandburg Family Trust. Illustrations copyright © 1998 by Anita Lobel. All rights reserved. Published in the United States by Alfred A. Knopf, Inc., New York, and simultaneously in Canada by Random House of Canada Limited, Toronto. Distributed by Random House, Inc., New York http://www.randomhouse.com/ *Library of Congress Cataloging-in-Publication Data* Sandburg, Carl, 1878–1967. Not everyday an aurora borealis for your birthday : a love poem / by Carl Sandburg ; pictures by Anita Lobel. p. cm. Summary: With great difficulty a young man brings his sweetheart an aurora borealis for a birthday present to show his love for her. ISBN 0-679-88170-0 (trade). — ISBN 0-679-88169-7 (pbk.). — ISBN 0-679-98170-5 (lib. bdg.) 1. Auroras—Juvenile poetry. 2. Birthdays—Juvenile poetry. 3. Children's poetry, American. [1. Auroras—Poetry. 2. Birthdays—Poetry. 3. American poetry.] I. Lobel, Anita, ill. II. Title. PS3537.A618N67 1998 811'.52—dc20 96-41685 Printed in Singapore 10 9 8 7 6 5 4 3 2 1

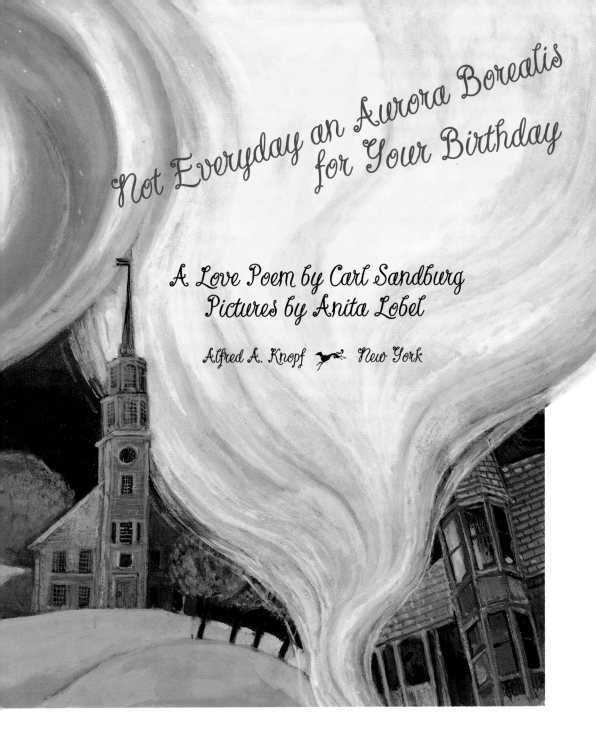

Not Everyday an Aurora Borealis for Your Birthday

A Love Poem by Carl Sandburg
Pictures by Anita Lobel

Alfred A. Knopf · New York

*I*t is because I love you I give you for a birthday present the aurora borealis.

It was a long trip I took carrying the aurora borealis to you.

Slippery is the aurora borealis. You think you have hold of it—

but it is sliding away off your hands and shoulders
and you have to stop and get a better hold on it.

Many times it came near getting away from me.

But I struggled with it and went on struggling . . .

till at last I laid on your doorstep, on your front porch,

stretching high into the sky, that fine big stack of shimmering
swimmering lights, that good old reliable aurora borealis.

When you want another aurora borealis you tell me

and I will go where the aurora borealises grow . . .

and I will struggle and go on struggling

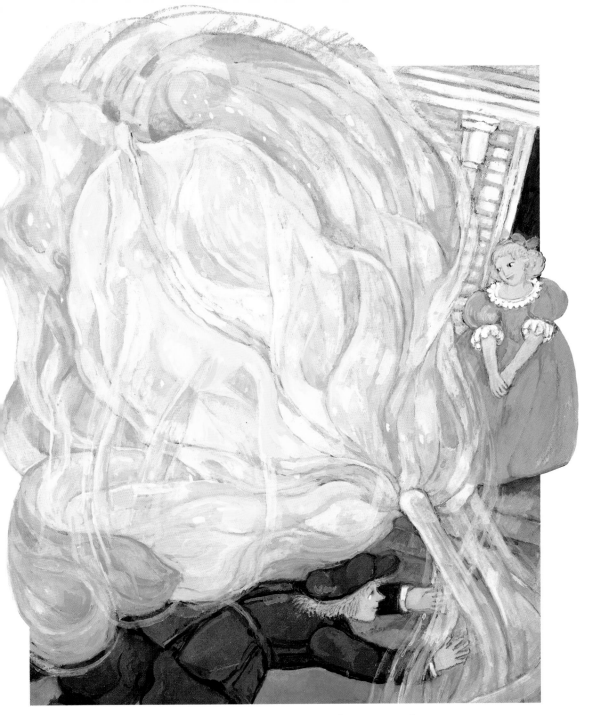

till I lay on your doorstep, on your front porch,
    one more aurora borealis, to show I love you.

And if you write to me saying you would like to have…

a big rainbow fresh off the sky,

I will struggle and go on struggling till you see it right there on your doorstep,

your front porch. You can see I am a struggler
        ready any day to struggle on to show you I love you.